ABYSS
part I

written, illustrated, & designed by Lucas Powers

ISBN 978-1-7341897-0-4 (hardback)
ISBN 978-1-7341897-2-8 (paperback)
ISBN 978-1-7341897-1-1 (ebook)

This book is dedicated to those who wonder what lie
under the veil of darkness, whether it be out of fear
or intrigue.

And to my parents, who have supported my journey
of getting here since the beginning.

Table of Contents

What do you see in the dark?

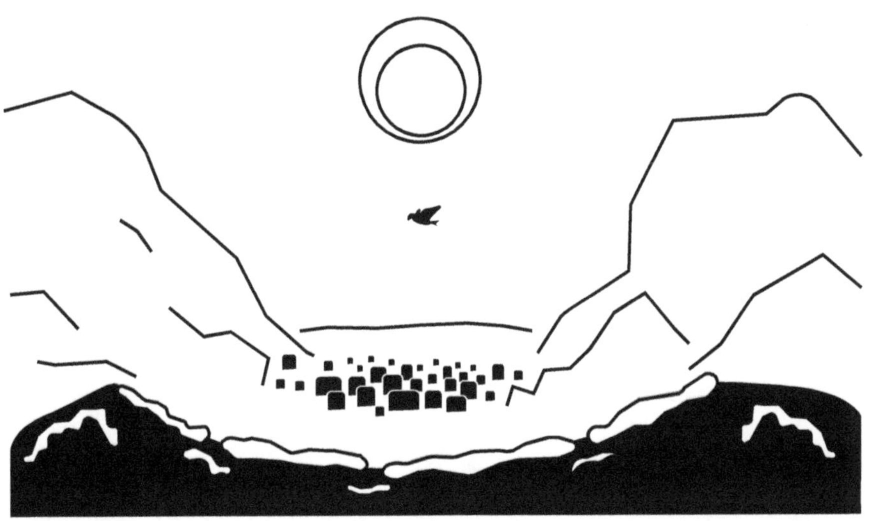

In a place just shy of nowhere sits a small town nuzzled between cliffs overlooking the great abyss. Day and night it roars, creating a feeling of place that not many towns can provide. The air is fresh, the people are happy, and the view is infinite. The adults work until the sun goes down while the children fill the sea breeze with laughter and joy.

There is a single road that leads to the town, and if one was to leave this utopia they would be forced to travel through a darker, taller abyss. The locals call it the Black Grove. This place evokes the same sort of awe as the ocean, but most avoid it because of the mystery its darkness hides. The trees block out the sound of the ocean, and in its place is a silence that is only occasionally interrupted by the sounds of life within. Creatures large and small live here, and even some humans that work in town find life more peaceful in the shade of the trees.

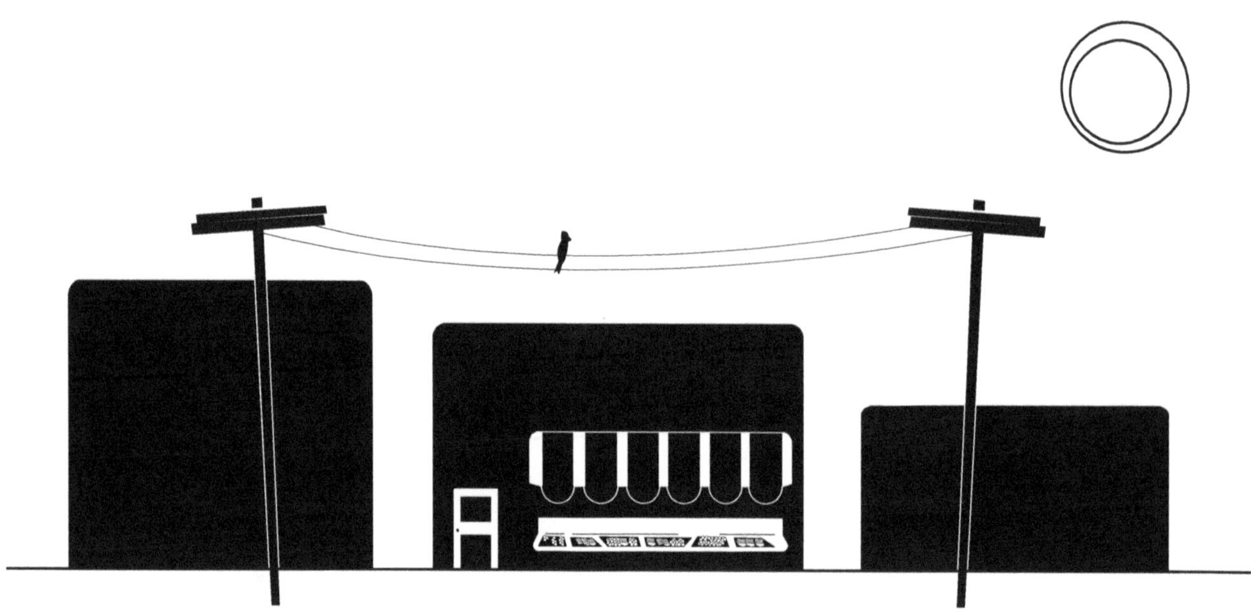

I am much like the humans. I spend my days in the town admiring the beautiful sweets and savory snacks of the market, waiting for one to fall off a shelf, or find its way through the fingers of a clumsy child. I enjoy the view of the ocean, and play with friends while the sun is up,

but at night I travel through the Black Grove to a place
that I call home.Its safe here. Its safe because of my
human. Her name is Sia.

Sia is different from the other humans. She feeds me, and loves me, and treats me different than everyone else. She even gave me a name. She calls me Kai. She's not scared of what I am.

We used to go to town together with her family.
We would play in the park while grandmother
watched, and her parents talked with other adults.
When the sun sank into the abyss and the sky started to bleed we would go back home through the
shade of the Black Grove.

But one day her parents disappeared.
Sia and Grandmother waited, but they never
came home. Sia said the Black Grove took them.
Grandmother said not to worry.

Sia doesn't leave the house anymore. She says the
Black Grove will take her too if she leaves.

Sia has fear now.

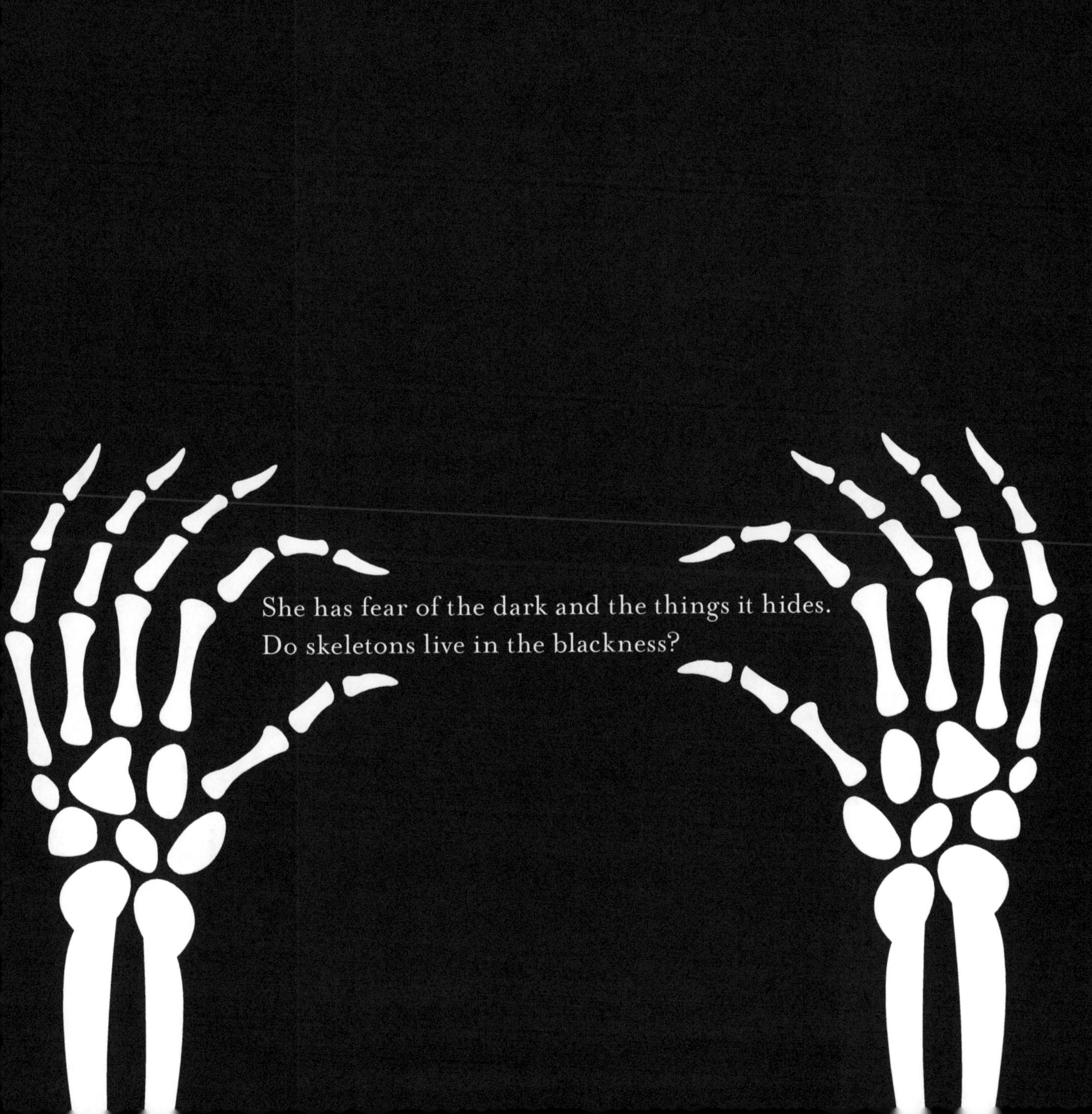
She has fear of the dark and the things it hides.
Do skeletons live in the blackness?

She has fear of the creaks and groans the house makes
at night. Is it the sound of ghosts creeping about?

She has fear of the mother spider and her children
who live in the house. Why are they so different from
the rest of us?

And above all she has fear of the outside.

Where did her parents go?

Weeks after Sia's parents disappeared

Kai!
Time for dinner!

Did you find them?

Its okay.
We will look tomorrow.
Are you hungry?

 Still no food… We are going to starve if Grandmother doesn't do something soon.

 I'm so hungry. We have one more can of "Maggotmeal." Would you find it while I check on Grandmother?

Grandmother?
We need food...

She's not going to help us Kai.

 You are in for a treat, little bird. Tonight we are watching a special movie.

 It's rated "S" for scarring. Momma would have never let me watch this, but it's Fathers favorite movie. I hope you're not a scaredy cat behind all of those feathers.

A storm is rolling in tonight.
Those on the coast are advised to stay in.
AND NOW...

WEATHER ALERT!

MIDNIGHT MONSTERS
OF
MOUNT MISCHIEF!

This is how most nights go.

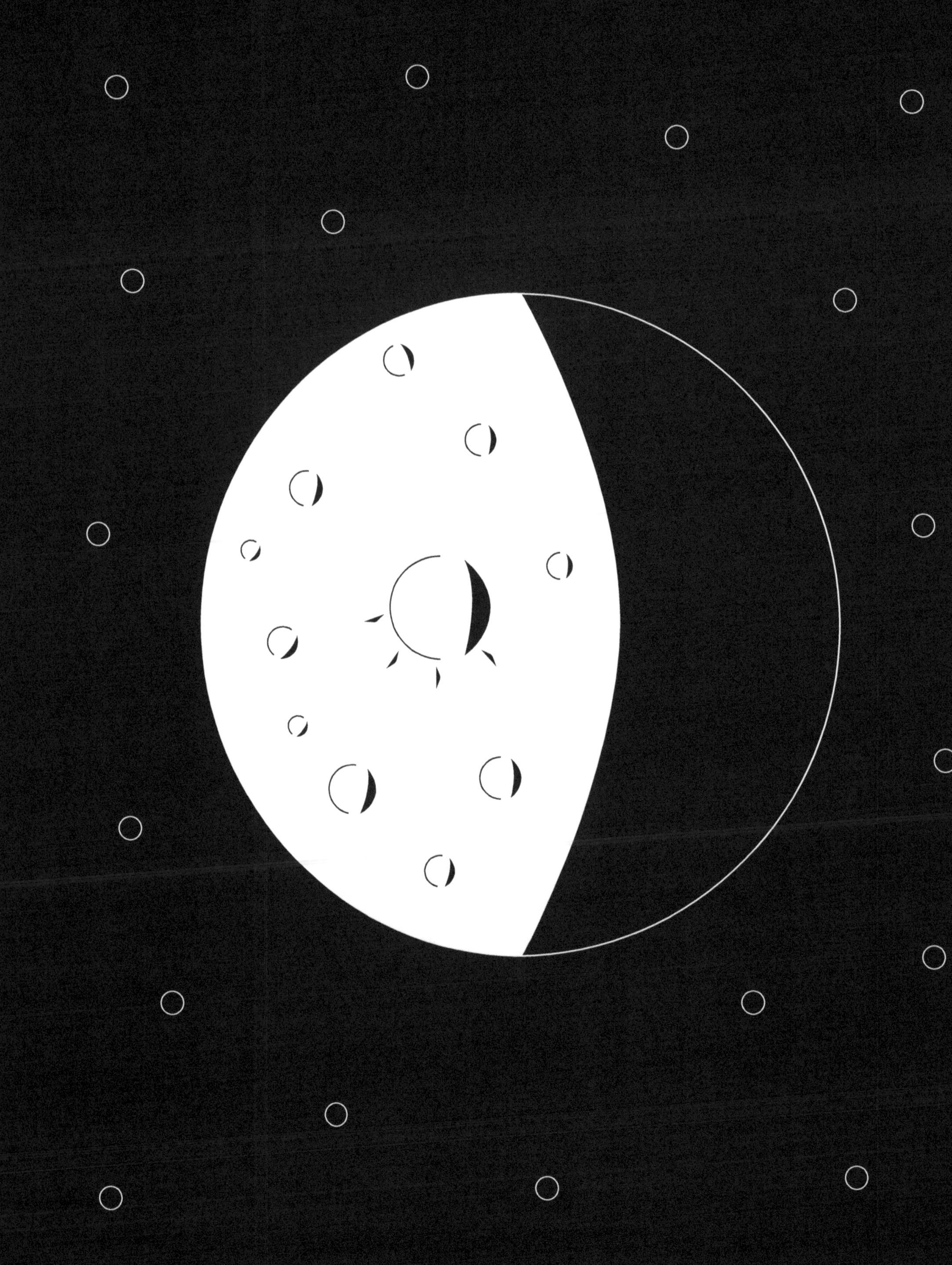

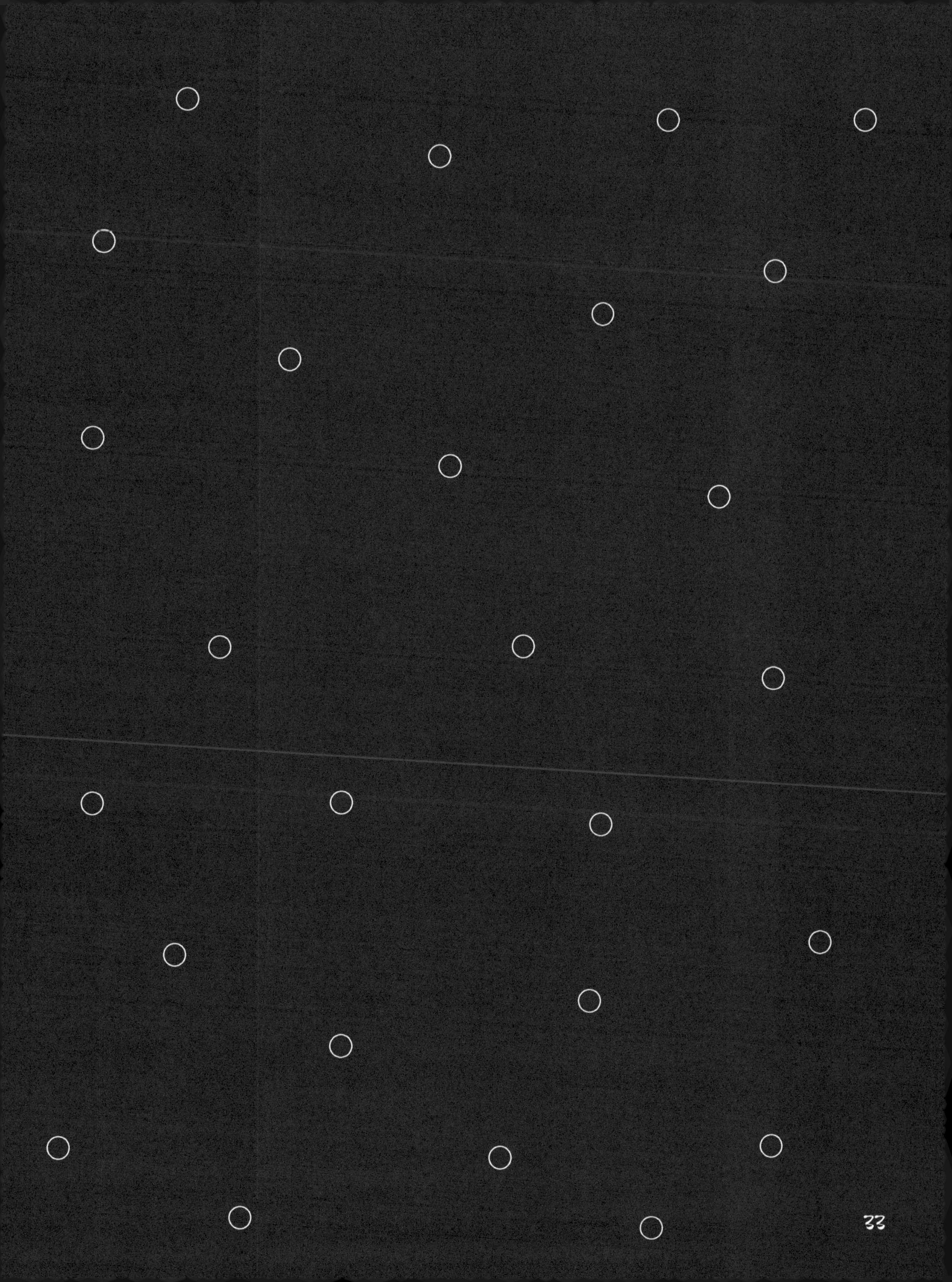

Grandmother won't leave her room, leaving only me
to help Sia face her fears when the world goes dark.

Thankfully the moving picture box helps her forget.

It's odd Sia is scared of so much, but these monster movies put her right to bed.

As the night progressed a storm brewed outside. A few drops
quickly grew to a million, and as the time drew closer to three
I could feel something more was coming.

CRACK!

I'm Scared Kai. Where are you?

Tap
Tap

Knock!
Knock!
Knock!

 Who would knock at this time of night?
Do you think it's Mother? Do you think
it's Father?

...

If its a monster you need to tell it to leave, okay?

Thats not Mother or Father...

It must
be a
monster...

Hello? Please, I need help! I'm cold and
wet and lost.

 Do monsters usually sound distressed?
Do you think it's trying to trick us?

 Please, this isn't a trick.

 Didn't you hear the "News Lady?" She said not to go outside tonight.

Who are you? Where did you come from?
Where are your parents?

My
name...
My name is
Alf —

I don't know what happened, or how I got here. I remember being home. Mom and Dad were getting ready to take me to see that new movie, "Slaughterly"…

They were happy. I remember hearing them laugh and joke from my room. Then I heard nothing. I peaked in their room and they were gone.

They disappeared?

The only thing left was their shoes sitting in front of the standing mirror. But the mirror... The mirror didn't show my reflection when I came close. All I saw was a forest. It was big and dark, and it looked like someone was standing in the shade of the trees, but I could only see a pair of eyes, glowing like the moon.

 The more I looked at those eyes the bigger they got, until all I could see was them. Everything went white, and then I was here.

 The eyes took you? Do you think the person in the woods took your parents? Do you think they are still out there?

 It all sounds crazy I know, but there isn't another way to explain it.

They wouldn't have just left me.

I believe you.
My parents disappeared too.

 It was a typical day. Grandmother and I were gathering our things to go to town. Mother and Father were working in the studio out back. They like making furniture, they even made this house. They were almost done making something for my room. They said they were going to meet us in town so they could finish it and set it up. Grandmother and I waited by the ocean till after the sun went down, but they never came.

 The thing they made for my room was
sitting at the bottom of the stairs when we
got home. They called it a vanity I think.
That was the only thing out of place.

And
now you
live
here alone?

No.
Kai lives here
and so does
Grand...

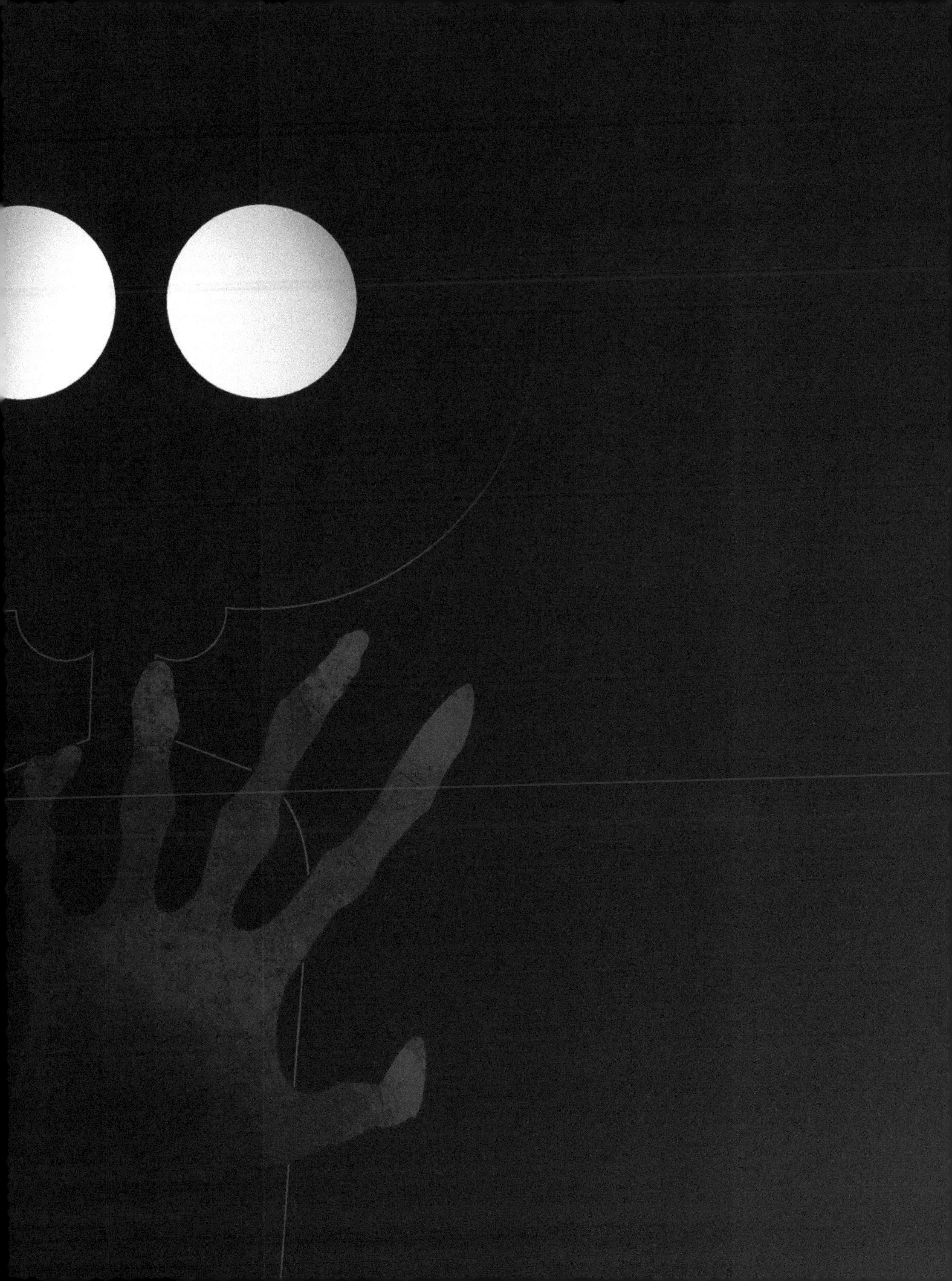

Who
is your
friend
little larva?

Hi im Alf. Sia saved me from the storm.

Don't you think it's a bit late little larva? I think your friend should go home now...

But Grandm...

I'm going upstairs, and I hope not to hear of this again.

She
seems
nice ...
!

 She hasn't been the same since Mother and Father left. I apologize, and don't worry you can stay here tonight. We just have to be quite.

Ever since the parents disappearance Sia's grandmother has started acting more and more odd.
She's lost the warm light that grandmothers have.

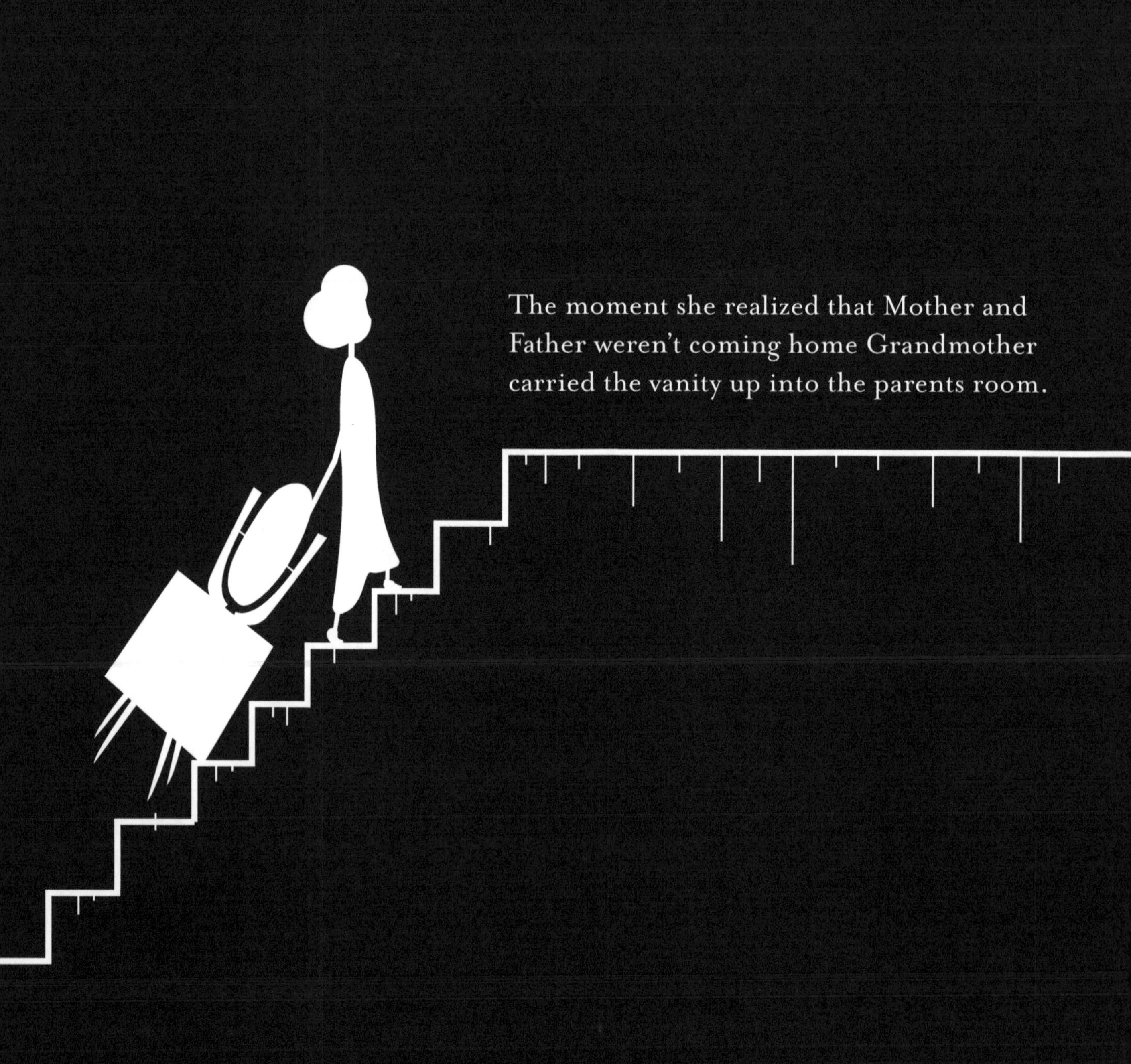

The moment she realized that Mother and Father weren't coming home Grandmother carried the vanity up into the parents room.

She hardly leaves that room now, and spends most of her time in front of the mirror held by the vanity. I haven't even seen her eat. She just stands there day and night staring at her refection.

Alf is an oddity as well. He seems sincere, and he's surprisingly chipper considering his situation, but how did he end up here?

Does he really think his parents disappeared through a mirror? Did he really travel through that mirror? Are his parents out in the woods somewhere too?

Is there a connection between grandmothers obses-
sion with her reflection and Alf's parents vanishing?

Did Sia's parents get taken by a mirror too?

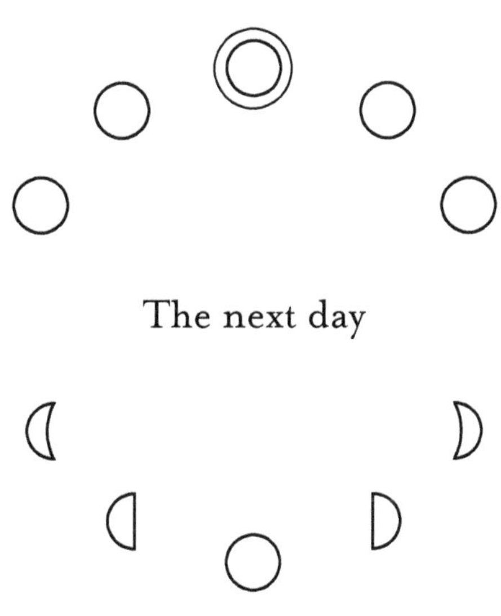

The next day

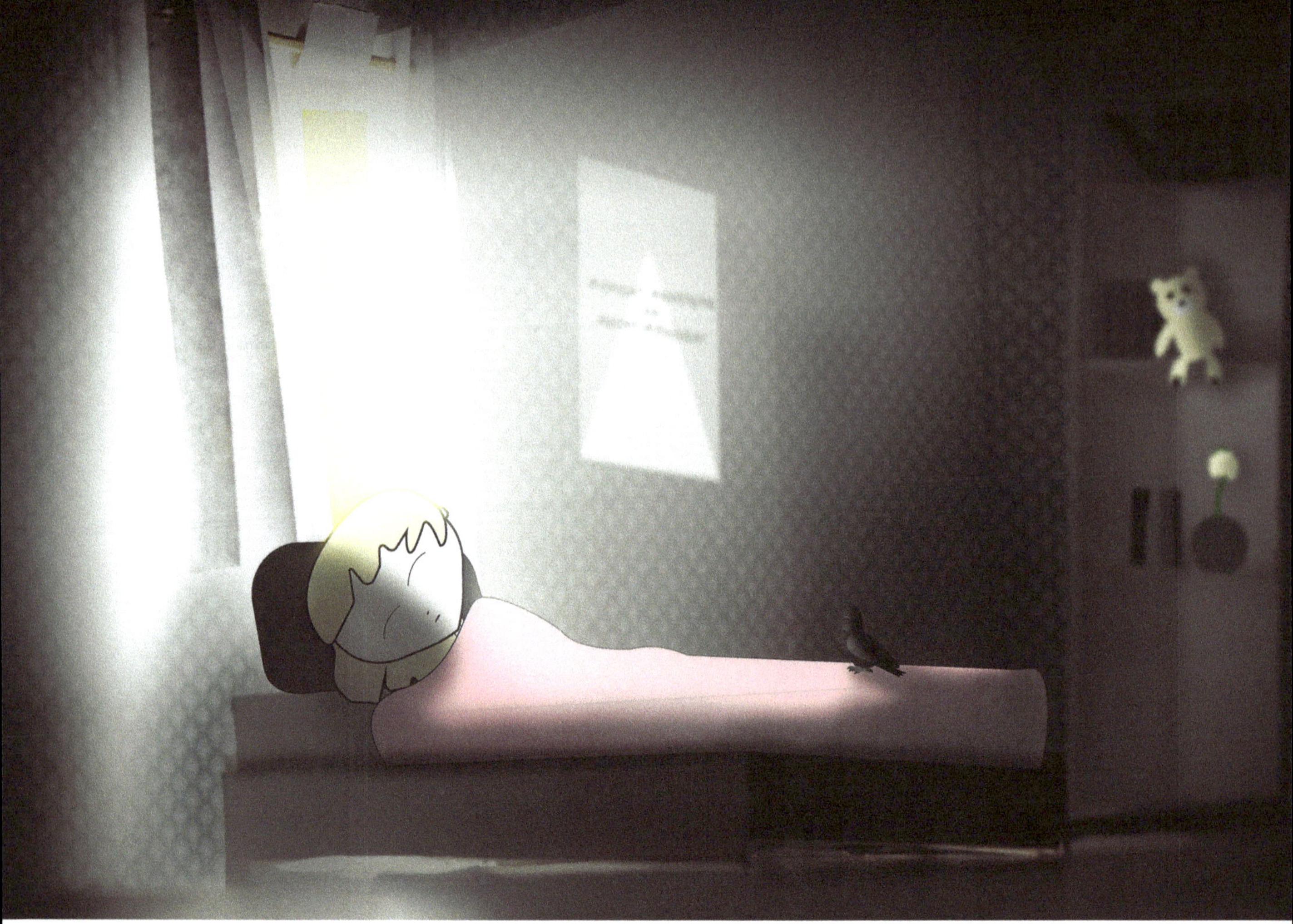

 Hey Sia? Are you awake?

I am now.

Mornin'
"little larva."

Is there any food? I haven't eaten since yesterdays lunch and I think my stomach is starting to eat my body.

No. Kai and I ate the last bit we had yester-day. We need Grandmother to go to town. I'll go check on her.

Grandmother?

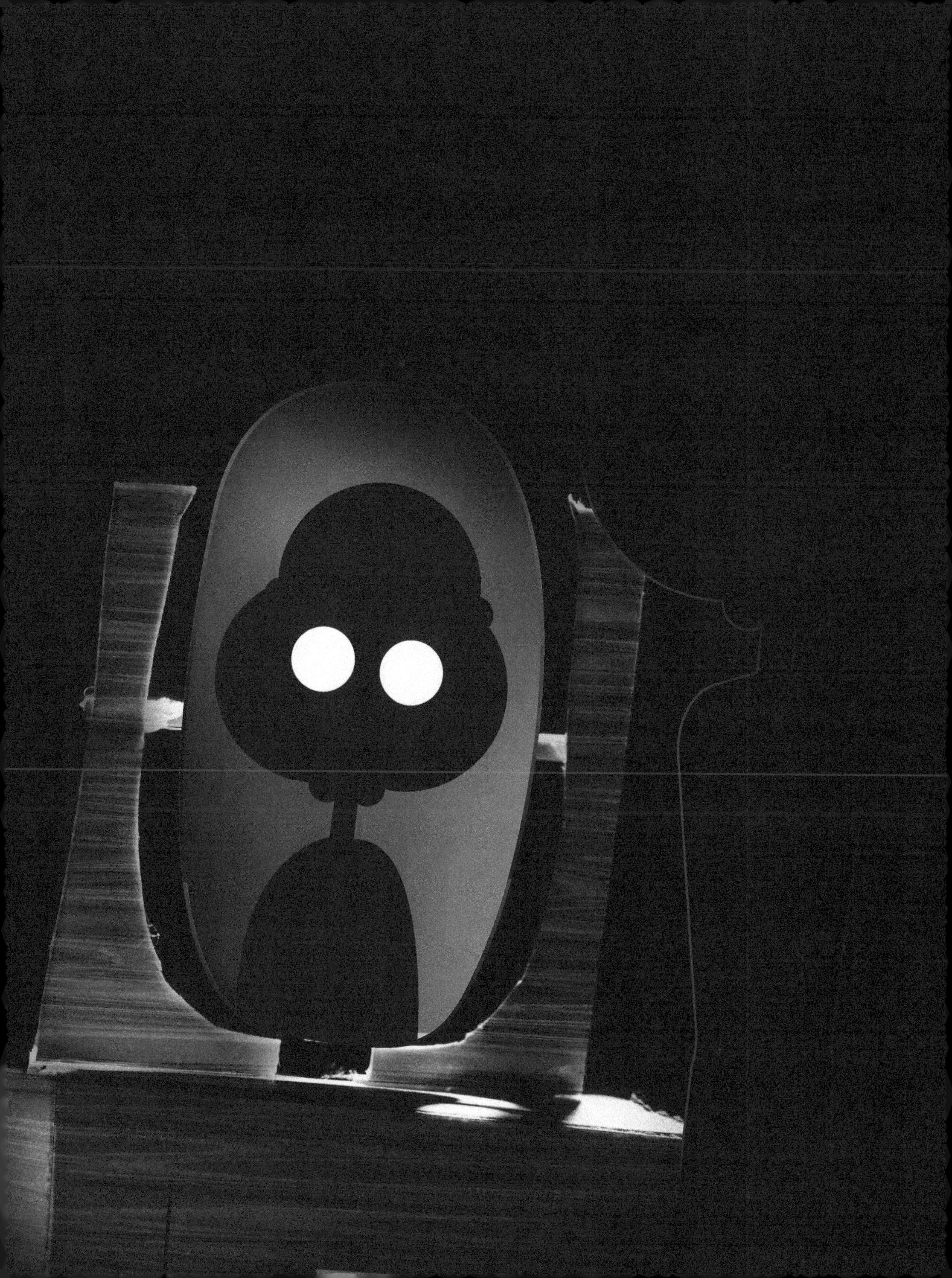

We need food. We have nothing.
Could you please go to town today?

Please Grandmother. We won't last the
week with nothing to eat.

Do you have any money?

No, but I know where Mother keeps the special day fund. Why? 

Why don't we go to town? We can't save our parents on an empty stomach.

I can't.

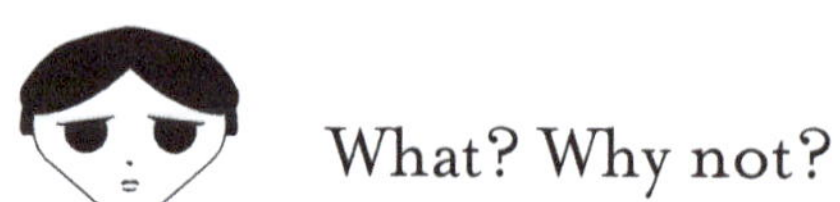

What? Why not?

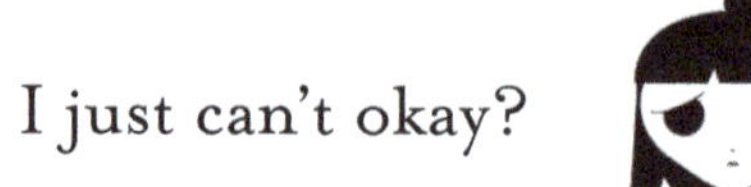

I just can't okay?

I don't understand. We can't just sit here and starve. We can't let our parents go un-found. We can't just do nothing!

I can't go outside. What if whatever took our parents is still out there? What if they take us next? I don't want to disappear too.

I'm not sure about your parents, but mine were taken by the thing in the mirror. It happened inside my own home. If any-thing, we are in more danger in here.

But... Well I don't know if that's what happened to mine.

All I know is that a mirror got me here, and ...

And...
what?

Are you
scared
of that
too?

AHHHHH!

You know these little things aren't nearly
as scary as they make them out to be.

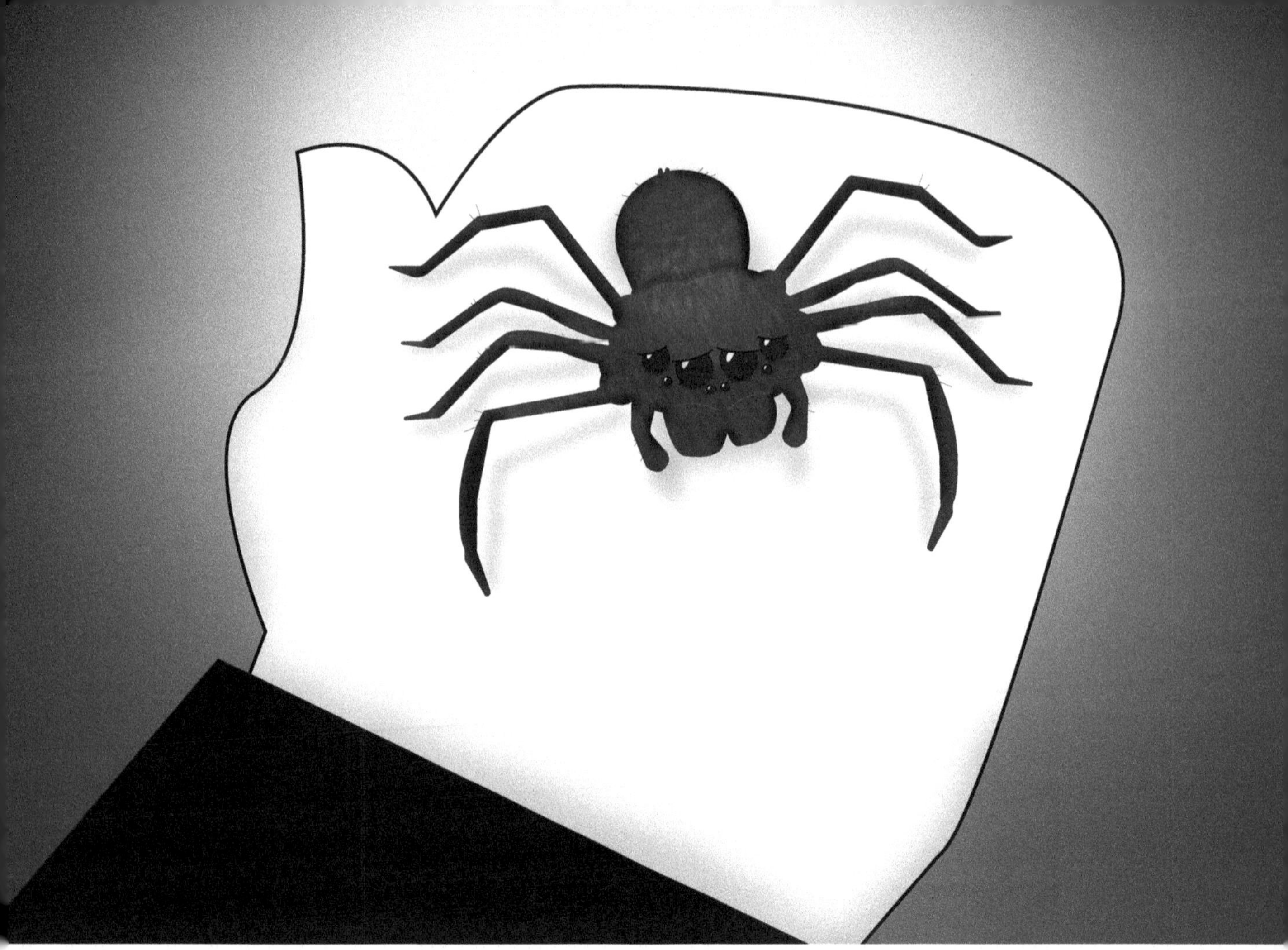

She wouldn't hurt a fly… I mean she would eat a fly, but it wouldn't hurt anything bigger than a fly. Why are you scared of it? Because you were told to be?

No! I don't like them. They are so different. I don't know what it would do, it might bite me or lay eggs in my ears! That scares me!!!

So the only reason your scared of it is because you don't know what it'll do?

 Yes.

 That's stupid.

 You're stupid.

 At least I'm not a "Tearful Fearful."

 Thats not even a thing.

 Yes it is. I just made it a thing, and it's what you are.

The two bickered all morning.

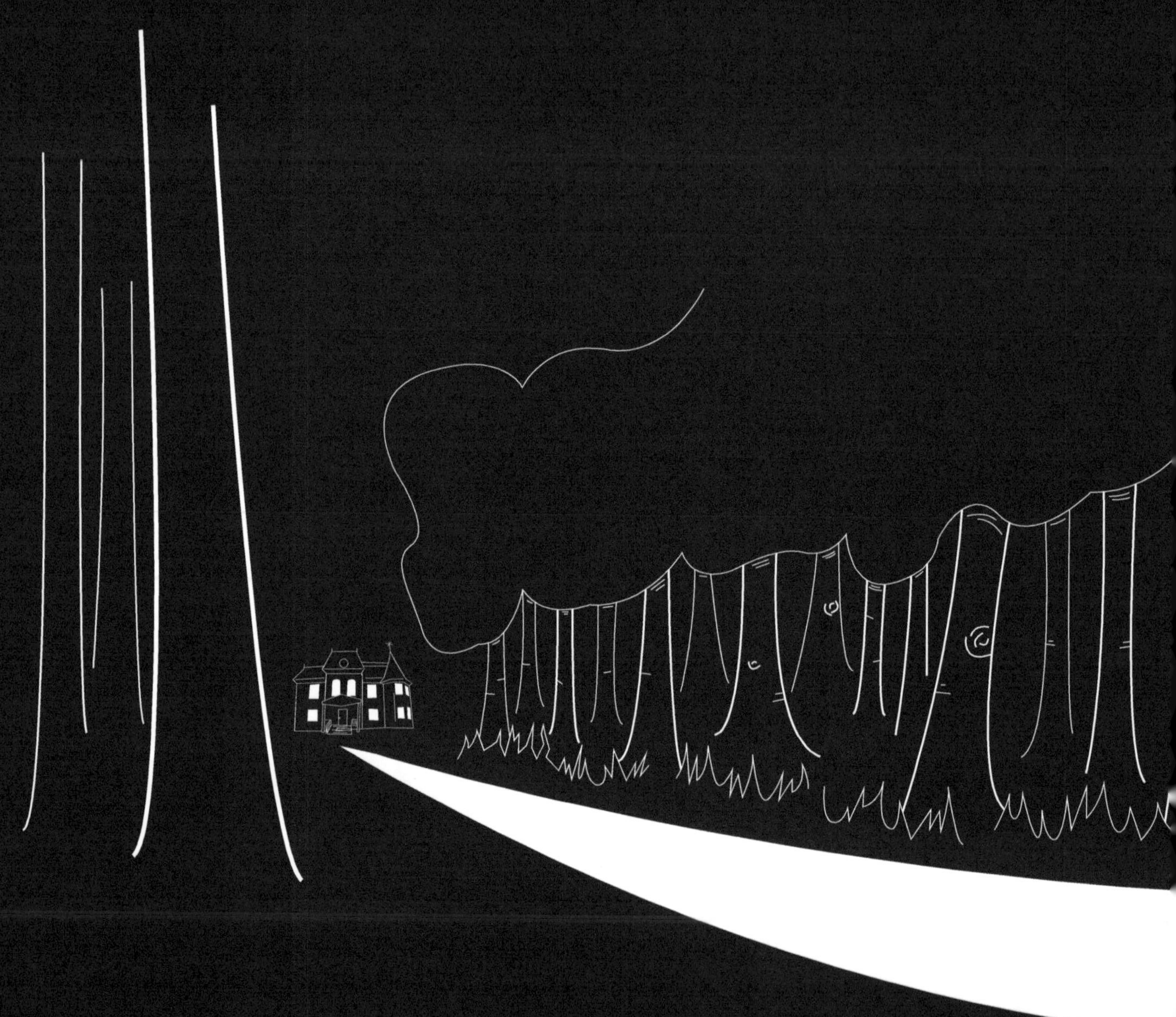

I decided to fly to town and look for food.
The weather still felt unsettled from the storm.
The breeze fought against every beat of my wings,
and the rain seemed to come and go.

Luckily I had the Black Grove to keep me dry.

The town felt lifeless today. Everyone must have been inside waiting for the clouds to clear. Not even my friends were out.

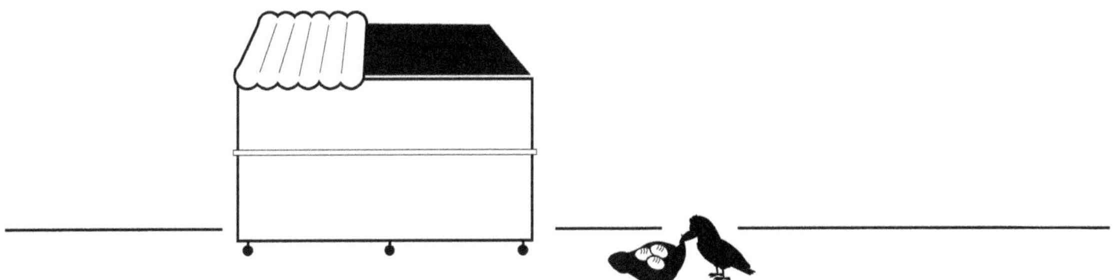

It worked in my favor though, as I was able to find some old bread thrown out by the baker. Usually he would shoo me off. With a little luck I even found something to carry a few rolls in. I hoped this would help with the hunger back home.

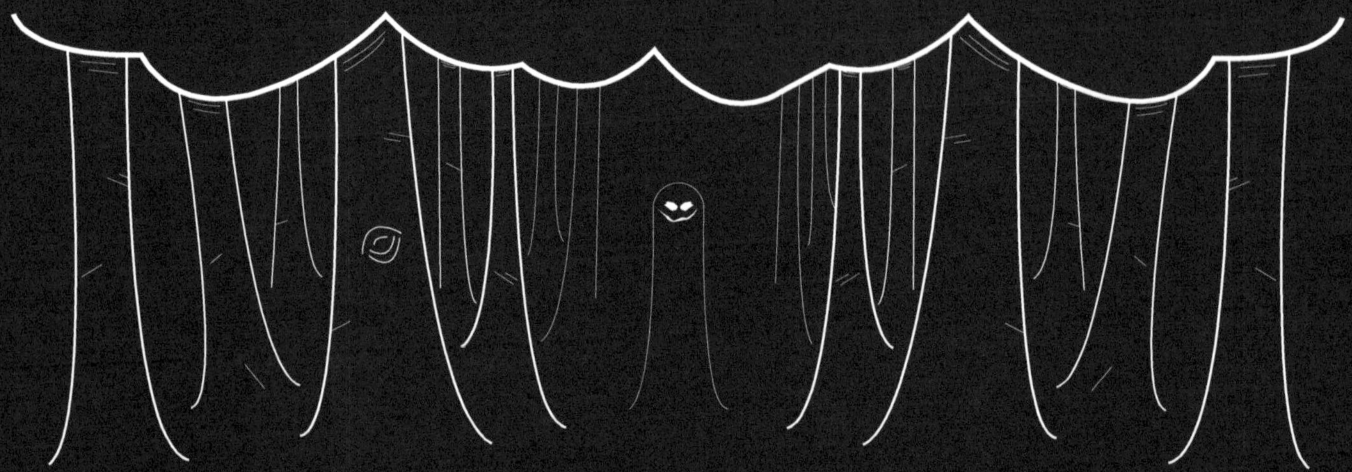

On my way back I encountered a creature in the
Black Grove I hadn't seen before. At first I thought it
was a person, so I flew closer to see if it could be one
of the parents. As I approached it started to look
more like a shadow, but the odd thing was it was
standing. It was as dark as the night, but it had these
eyes that illuminated the space around it.

When I got close enough it lashed out at me and
ripped the cloth carrying the food. I lost two of the
rolls, but was able to carry one home. I could feel its
eyes watch me all the way back.

Not much had changed when I got home.

Alf was still curious about Sia's fears, and he seemed to be enjoying testing her. This could be good for her though. If we are to find her parents she must conquer her fear of leaving the house.

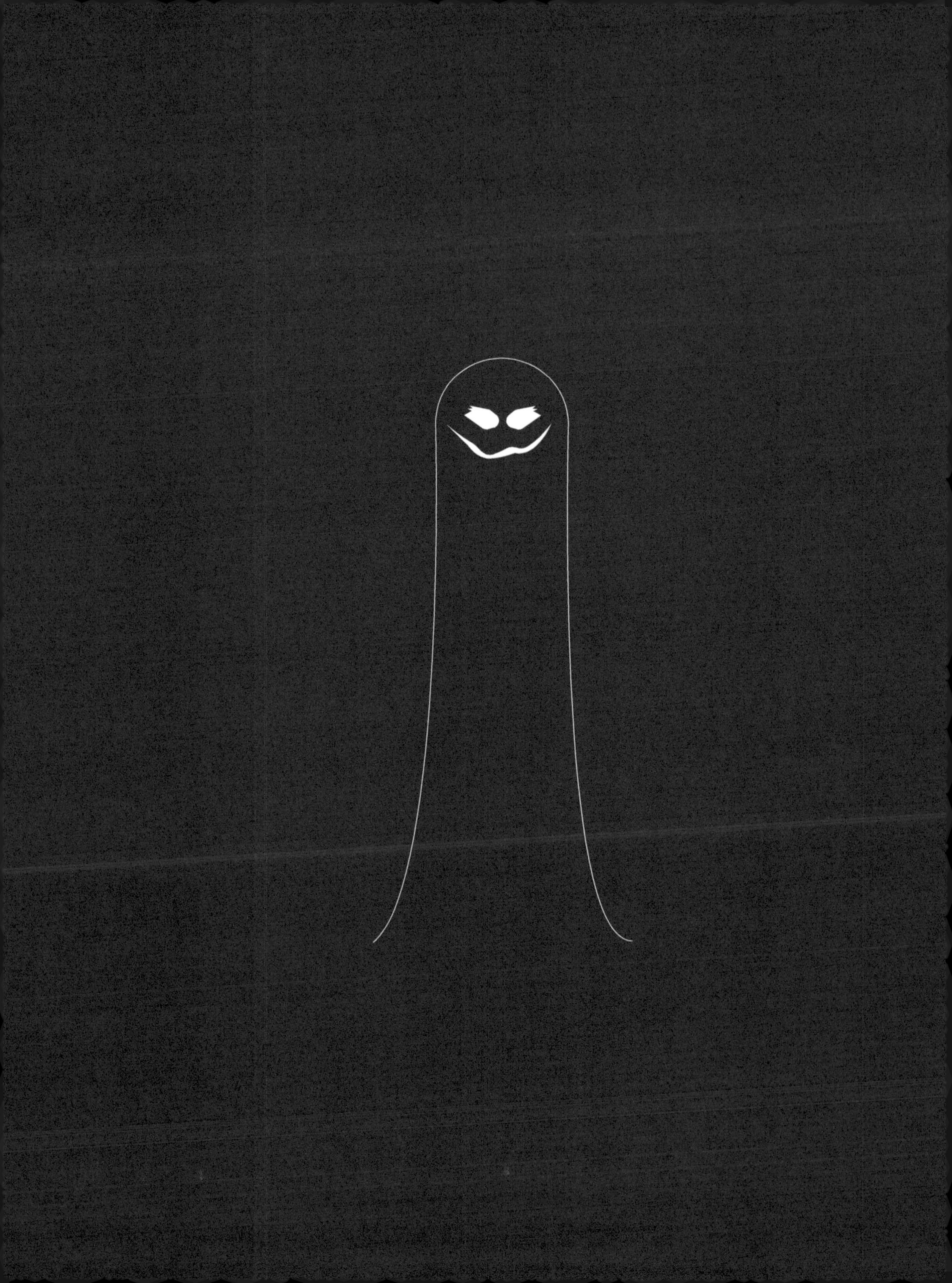

Was that the thing Alf saw in the mirror?

 So let me get this straight. You're scared
of the dark, the noises your house
makes, the attic, the basement, things
with a lot of holes, feet, spiders and
most bugs, plastic wrap, sharp objects,
and the outside?

Pomegranates? Are you serious? What makes a pomegranate scary?

I know this one's silly, but it's the color of the inside. And all the seeds. And the skin inside. It's like a human brain or something. It's like…

No please, don't go on. Just because something's gross doesn't mean you have to be scared of it. It's not like it's going to kill you.

Maybe…

 No Sia. Fear comes from the unknown, it's like the main part of it, ya know? You can't be scared of the pomegranate because you already know whats going to happen. It's going to look like a brain inside and taste delicious, and that's it.

I just don't know... 

 Well we need to get you to know, and quick. Im hungry and I want to eat. So we need to...

A single roll? I guess it's a start. Thank you Kai. Now like I was saying, lets start working on your fears.

No, I don't want to do any of that. 

My parents and my stomach are on the line here Sia. YOUR parents and YOUR stomach are too.

... 

 Is this really how you want to die? Starved in a dark house with a weird old lady upstairs? Kai would probably eat your brain if you died in here.

...

Okay. I guess we can try.

Oh Yeah! I can taste the food now! Does your town have good food?

Yes. Very good actually. Just don't get the stew from "Riddlies Riddler." They put seagulls in it.

I'd eat anything at this point! Okay so what should we familiarize you with first? ... Lets do plastic wrap and sharp things, and we'll work our way up from there. Okay?

Okay.

The two spent the whole day working on Sia's fears. I have to admit, Alf is a persistent one.

The plastic wrap was a breeze. She just had to turn Alf into a plastic mummy, and after a good laugh she seemed much more comfortable with it.

Sharp objects came second. Alf brought in some sticks,
and he taught her how to whittle. Like the plastic wrap,
it just took some perspective to help ease the fear.

When it came to feet, she was a bit hesitant. Alf said
she could tickle him with her toes, but only if she
painted them. She painted her toenails for the first
time, and Alf helped.

She couldn't come to terms with things that have a lot of holes, although alf tried his best. He got the pasta strainer and made it into a helmet that she had to wear. She didn't last long.

And then it came to the basement.

I don't think
I can do this.

 Your going to be fine. Trust me. Unless of course you have a basement monster. Then we are doomed to die.

Your not helping. 

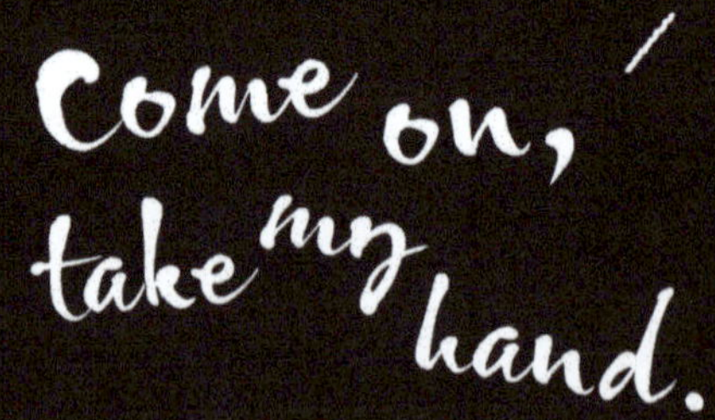

Alright. Three, two, GO!

WAIT!

For what?

I'm not ready.

 You'll never be ready at this rate.

... 

These monsters better look out!

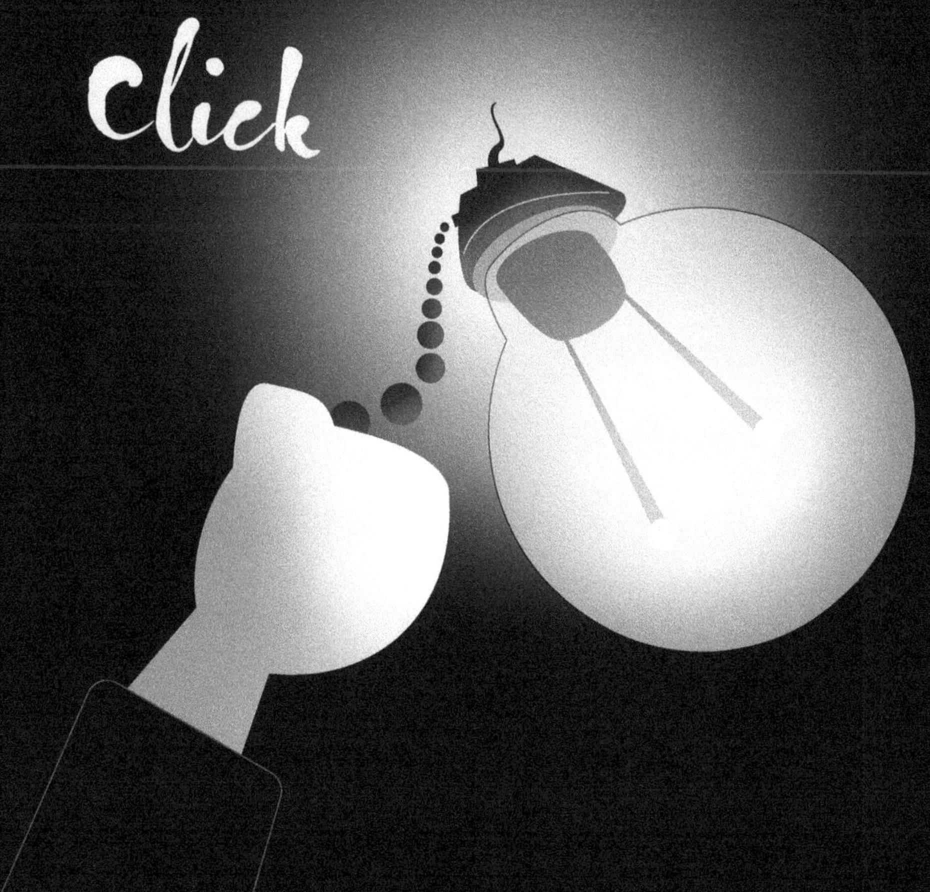
Click

See,
not so bad right?

POP!

I've never seen a light explode like that…
But it's boring down here anyways.
Whats next on our list of fears?

… 

How about the attic!

But thats where the mother spider lives… 

Perfect! Two birds with one stone!

 It smells weird up here.

Yeah, one of the many reasons I don't come up here. 

Look at all this stuff!

This place is awesome! If this was my house I'd totally make it my fort.

Yeah I guess. Everything is so dusty though. 

It's like a museum! Remind me again why you don't like it up here?

It's all the hidden areas and dark corners. It feels like something is hiding. 

The only thing hiding up here is our imagination!

I suppose some of this stuff is kind of neat.

That's Mother Spider. She's the reason
for all the spiders in the house. She's
been around as long as I have. She just
wont seem to die.

May I hold you?

No don't!

She's
beautiful.

 I've never seen something like you before.

I can't believe this is happening right now.
You are crazy! 

 She's friendly Sia. Here, hold her.

 No way in a fiery place I'm going to do that.

 Have I been wrong yet? Nothing that you were scared of ended up being actually scary. You make friends with the little mother spider, and then we go save our parents!

 … You're not going to give me a choice here are you?

Nope. 

There ya go, nice and slow. You don't want to scare her.

Scare her? What about me!

Stay steady Sia. You can open your eyes now.

She really is something ku?

Told you! Now bring her down stairs.

I'm not going to do that, but I am ready to go back down. Have you seen Kai? 

Not since the basement. He must be a bigger chicken than you.

He's a raven. 

There

he is.

What're you looking at Kai?

Isn't that your grandmas room? Should I stay back?

Thats the vanity my parents made. Where is Grandmother?

You see anything weird?

 Alf come here.

What is it? What do you see? 

 Wh-wh-what is that?

Thats the thing I saw in the mirror when my parents disappeared! Sia we need to get out of here!

 RUN! 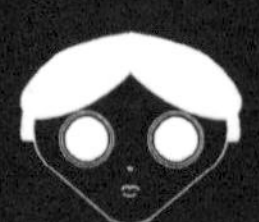

SLAM!

WHAT'RE WE GOING TO DO?!

...

ALF COME ON! I NEED YOU RIGHT NOW!

...

BANG!

BANG!

BANG!

...

BANG!

BANG!

BANG!

BANG!

BANG!

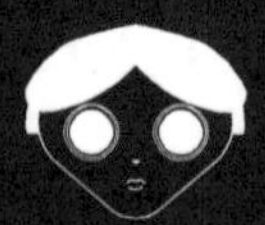
THATS A REAL MONSTER
OUT THERE ISN'T IT?!

YES! I'M GLAD WE ARE ON THE
SAME PAGE, NOW WHAT ARE WE
GOING TO DO?!

Okay okay hang on… How many
steps is your room from the
front door?

You think I count that?

GIVE ME A NUMBER SIA!

Twenty!

BANG!

BANG!

Am I? You were the one crying a second ago.

That doesn't matter right now. Right now we need to get out of this house. We need to get as far away from that thing as possible.

But…

No buts! You didn't want to leave the house because of what took your parents. That thing out there took your parents, IN YOUR HOUSE. We aren't safe here. Do you understand?

 Yes. What are we going to do though? It's right outside.

 We are too high up to use your window, so we have to go this way. I say we...

 I say we wait. It has to let up at some point. Who knows, maybe your grandma will show up. As soon as it's distracted we book it straight for the door. Can you forget about your fears for twenty steps?

 I can try. Where do we go then though?

 We go straight to town. Maybe someone can help us.

 I don't know what I'll do once I'm outside. Its been so long, but I guess it's all we can do.

 I believe in you Sia. Now we wait...

See
anything?

Looks clear to me. You ready?

As ready as I can be. Follow us Kai.

Twenty steps. Thats all it's going to
take. If it shows up we run past it, don't
look at it. Keep your eyes on the door.
Count us down.

THREE...TWO... GO!

Almost to
the stairs!

DON'T STOP JUST GO!

Almost there!

Do you see it? Is it following us?

No I don't think so, looks like we're in
the clear!

Hey Sia
wait up!

 What is it? Are you okay?

 Yeah. I just wanted to say welcome
back outside.

The children and I moved as fast as we could, but the
Black Grove seemed to draw on for eternity. With only
the moon to show our way we went from bits of light to
pitch black and back to light again. Luckily survival was
on the table, and adrenalin was the byproduct of that.
As we dived deeper into the woods I started to see what
looked like more of those dreadful glowing eyes, the
same eyes that creature from the mirror had. Luckily
the children didn't seem to notice, and it didn't affect
our journey.

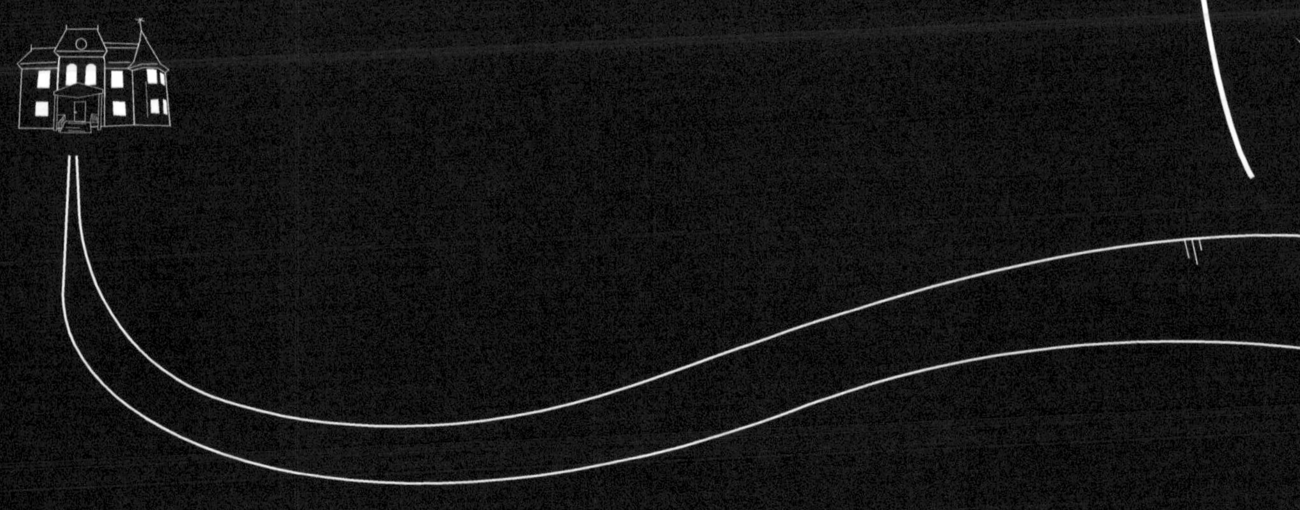

Crimson bled over the ocean abyss as we reached the
end of the Black Grove, and it induced a feeling
of serenity that I hadn't felt since before Sia's
parents disappeared.

The feeling was short lived though. The town felt just as lifeless as the day before. The quiet was so present that it made the streets of our home town feel almost foreign. We continued with caution to a store we knew would have remedies for the childrens hunger, and oddly enough we found the front door to be unlocked.

While they tended to their basic needs I was able to reflect on our last 48 hours. Sia was so dreadfully scared before Alf showed up. Her fearful tendencies ranged from sane to irrational, but despite how deep they ran, overcoming most of them was as simple as gaining a new perspective. Alf's insistence on confronting her fears was effective, and proved that exposure to something can alleviate so much of our worries. It would seem that fear by its very nature is something that accumulates within us when new information emerges, making the time to think and ponder the only real culprit in the matter. Fear comes from within ourselves, and is often more reflective of our own thoughts and feelings rather than reality.

Sadly, this clarity comes at the cost of many
unanswered questions.

Where did the children's parents go?
What was that dark figure in the mirror?
Why was Alf brought to us?
Where did Grandmother go?
What has happened to the town?

And most importantly, will Sia ever
overcome her fear of pomegranates?

Things have become very odd very fast, and I fear
that they will only become worse, but we are fed and
safe for the moment.

This will do for now.

A NOTE
FROM THE AUTHOR

Thanks for reading my first book!

This project started as an open ended senior thesis. It began with 3 months of research in the topic of my choosing. I used this time to investigate the development of fear in children. My primary research consisted of interviewing a wide range of individuals of varying backgrounds and ages, and my secondary research focused on the history of the horror genre and the nature of fear itself.

The second part of this thesis project was to take my data and communicate it visually. As a lover of dark narratives, and especially "kid friendly horror," I found the opportunity to try my hand at creating a story that could show information, rather than tell it. As I started to form a story arc I began to realized that world building, story telling, and illustration were all things I loved, and a book was the perfect way to combine these passions.

The story of ABYSS has just begun. I hope to see you deeper in the depths!

View my full portfolio at:
bylucaspowers.art

Say hi on instagram and prepare for upcoming projects at:
bylucaspowers